Books are to be returned on or before the last date below.

THE
QUEEN'S
HINGLISH
~~How to speak pukka~~

Baljinder K. Mahal

HarperCollins Publishers
Westerhill Road
Bishopbriggs
Glasgow G64 2QT

First Edition 2006
© HarperCollins Publishers 2006
www.collins.co.uk

Illustrations
© Sarah J Coleman

ISBN-13: 978-0-00-724112-5
ISBN-10: 0-00-724112-7

A catalogue record for this book is
available from the British Library.

Typeset in Martin Majoor's FF Nexus
by Wordcraft, Glasgow

Printed and bound by Legoprint SPA

ACKNOWLEDGEMENTS
We would like to thank those authors
and publishers who kindly gave
permission for copyright material
to be used in the Collins Word Web.
We would also like to thank Times
Newspapers Ltd for providing valuable
data. All rights reserved.

EDITOR: Cormac McKeown

William Collins' dream of knowledge for all began with the publication of his first book in 1819. A self-educated mill worker, he not only enriched millions of lives, but also founded a flourishing publishing house. Today, staying true to this spirit, Collins books are packed with inspiration, innovation, and practical expertise. They place you at the centre of a world of possibility and give you exactly what you need to explore it.

Language is the key to this exploration, and at the heart of Collins Dictionaries is language as it is really used. New words, phrases, and meanings spring up every day, and all of them are captured and analysed by the Collins Word Web. Constantly updated, and with over 2.5 billion entries, this living language resource is unique to our dictionaries.

Words are tools for life. And a Collins Dictionary makes them work for you.

Collins. Do more.

Contents

INTRODUCTION

English is and always has been a greedy language. Throughout the centuries it has been gathering exotic words from other tongues like a wildly successful gambler hoarding chips. As surely as each fresh chapter in its continuing adventures prompts a spate of gloomy predictions about its imminent demise, English keeps getting richer – its relentless appetite for the new making it at once the largest and most versatile of all the world's languages. Recently English has seen off perceived threats from the internet, email, and the mobile phone. But we don't all talk in 'disemvowelled' text-speak. The structure hasn't fallen apart; the word-hoard has merely got more impressive still. This book is an informal celebration of yet another development in the adventure of English, and one that the doomsayers won't like: the rise and rise of Hinglish.

More people speak English in South Asia than in Britain and North America combined. India alone accounts for more than 350 million English-speakers. Although the practice was previously frowned upon by purists, people there are becoming more and more comfortable with mixing words from languages such as Hindi, Urdu, and Punjabi with English, which is still the official language. This means that Hinglish, as this modern blend of standard English, Indian English, and South Asian languages is popularly known, could soon become the most widely spoken form of English on earth. The purists might object, but the purists – as they always do – have lost the battle. Hinglish, once seen as the lingo of the uneducated masses, is now trendy – the language of the movers and shakers. Of course this has not been lost on the marketing departments of the world's multinationals. Big companies are happy to promote their wares in catchy Hinglish taglines. Pepsi, for example, proclaims 'Yeh Dil Maange More!' (The heart wants more) while Coke, not to be outdone, counters with 'Life Ho To Aisi' (Life should be this way).

In the UK too, a variation on South Asian Hinglish is establishing itself. Where a sentence from its Subcontinental cousin might have a fairly even balance of Hindi and English elements, British Hinglish consists predominantly of English peppered with words from a South Asian language. And it's usually the same set of South Asian words that are selected; slang words, everyday words, family words. Words that are first to your lips when your son has taken the car again or your sister is wearing your trainers or food is so delicious it takes you by surprise. The entries in *The Queen's Hinglish* can be divided roughly into three main categories. The majority are words that are currently being assimilated into British English from Hindi, Urdu, and Punjabi, such as *apna*, *machi chips*, and *gora*. These three South Asian languages are the mostly widely spoken in Britain after English and consequently are the source for most British Hinglish words. Another type of entry lists those Hindi, Urdu, and Punjabi words which are commonly mixed into English on the South Asian subcontinent, for example *bustee, dai, char-sau-bees,* but which for various reasons have not yet made an impact on British English. The final class of entry deals with words and phrases peculiar to the branch of English used in South Asia, and which are a mixture of quaint throwbacks to another era, such as *stepney,* and new formations like *prepone* and *airdash.*

No-one is claiming that all the vocabulary in this book will be casually dropped into conversation over the average white British dinner table any time soon, merely that these words exist, and are being used every day by a huge number of Britons and South Asians while – and this is the critical thing – *they are speaking English.* As British *desis* increasingly make their voices heard in all areas of mainstream culture, these words, which are already become part of the overarching super-language that is World English, will become more and more familiar to an audience that even 10 years ago would have been hard pressed to think of a South Asian word that didn't stem from the time of the Raj, or from the local curry house. And the next generation of kids growing up in today's multicultural streets will be even more receptive to these novel additions to their broadening vocabulary, especially if there's the slightest chance their parents won't understand them...

Hinglish refers to mixing elements of South Asian languages, particularly Hindi, Urdu, and Punjabi, with English, where speakers switch between two languages within the same sentence.

Hindi

Hindi is the main official language of India, where it is primarily spoken in the northern and central regions. It is one of the world's most widely spoken languages: the mother tongue or second language of 480 million speakers in India, there are a further 320 million Hindi speakers around the world, particularly in Nepal, South Africa, Mauritius, Yemen, Uganda, Germany, New Zealand, Singapore, the UK, the US, and the UAE. Historically, Hindi is closely related to Urdu, belonging to the same language family. These languages are so similar in structure that they could be considered to be dialects of the same language. However, the vocabulary of the two languages is quite different, particularly formal and literary words, with many words of Hindi taken from Sanskrit, in contrast to the greater influence of Persian and Arabic borrowings on Urdu. Some examples of words derived from Hindi which have been commonly mixed with English in informal situations are: *bacha* (child), *desi* (local), and *kunjoos* (mean).

Urdu

Urdu is the official language of Pakistan, along with English, and parts of India including Jammu and Kashmir, Delhi, Uttar Pradesh, and Andhra Pradesh, totalling 61 million native speakers. Besides these regions of Southern

Asia, it is spoken by a further 43 million native speakers in the Persian Gulf, Saudi Arabia, the UK, the US, Canada, Australia, and Norway. While Urdu and Hindi are from the same language family, Urdu has borrowed a greater number of words from Persian and Arabic than are found in Hindi and is written in a different script. Many Urdu terms which have been borrowed into English are well-established, for example *masala,* which in Hinglish has developed the new sense 'spicy' or 'dramatic'.

Punjabi
As the official language of the state of Punjab and Chandigarh in India, Punjabi is spoken by an estimated 30 million people, as well as 80 million speakers in Pakistan. Around the world, Punjabi is spoken by large immigrant communities in the UK, the US, Canada, and Australia. Punjabi is from the same language family as Urdu and Hindi, and is thought to be the closest of these to the original Sanskrit, though it has also been influenced by Persian and Arabic. It differs from other Northern Indian languages in that it is tonal, an aspect which may have arisen through contact with Chinese during its development. Punjabi is written in two different scripts using the Gurmukhi alphabet and the Shahmukhi alphabet. Some very evocative words have been absorbed into Hinglish from the strong Punjab literary tradition, such as *Ranjha* (male lover), from the love story of *Heer Ranjha.* Other Hinglish words from Punjabi are *pendu* (culturally backward) and *teek* (in good health).

HOW TO USE THIS BOOK

The Queen's Hinglish *is designed with easy browsing in mind. Most of it is self-explanatory – you don't have to read the following to enjoy the book but here is some information to help you get the most out of it.*

• Headwords

All main entries, including acronyms and abbreviations, are printed in magenta boldface type and are listed in strict alphabetical order, with any common variant spellings given after the headword:

bevakoof *or* **befkoof** *noun* a fool

• Labels

The standard parts of speech are presented in labels preceding the sense or senses relating to that part of speech. Where one word can be used as more than one part of speech, the change is indicated by the symbol |

doosra *adjective* **1** second … | *noun* *cricket* **2** a delivery …

A noun or interjection that is commonly used as if it were an adjective is labelled (*as modifier*):

Bollywood… **2** *as modifier*: a Bollywood star

If a particular sense of a word is resticted as to appropriatenes, connotation subject field, region, etc, an italic label is given:

chak de phatte *interjection informal* an exhortation to be joyful ...

• *Derivations*
Words derived from a headword by the addition of suffixes such as -ly, -ness, etc, are presented in boldface type. They are preceded by the symbol > and the meaning of each can be deduced from that of the relevant headword:

fob *noun* ... > **fobby** *adjective*

• *Examples of use*
Every entry is supported by a citation from our diverse range of sources, illustrating both its currency and how it is used in today's English.

> bhangra is most probably the closest thing India has to dance music and, and despite its reputation for livening up a party with its trademark 'chak de patte' slogan ... its lyrics are often rooted in gritty social realism reflecting life in Punjabi communities *(The Guardian)*

Spellings and pronunciations

When words from South Asian languages are represented in Roman characters the spellings are chosen to reflect the sound of the words in their original language, rather than to adhere to a definitive set of rules; such a standard for spellings does not yet exist. Their representations in Roman characters are written to reflect pronunciation. A few words, especially those – such as *aashique* – that feature heavily in Bollywood film titles, subtitles, and promotional material have taken on quasi-conventional spellings. Where these exist we have given them; for other entries we have simply provided the most common spellings occurring in our sources.

When talking about Hinglish as a whole, pronunciation is a fairly fluid concept. One person could very well pronounce the same word differently depending on the language in which the rest of the sentence is set out. If, for example *badmash* was dropped into an English sentence, its pronunciation would often be closer to that of a normal English word that it would be if it was used in a purely Hindi sentence. The same person might use that same word again within an otherwise English sentence, but this time give a much more *desi* pronunciation, depending on the context, the person being addressed, and so on. With this variance in mind, combined with the fact that pronunciations differ greatly from region to region, we have decided not to attempt to formalize them in each entry. Having said that, a few generally observed conventions are worth noting.

'A's in South Asian languages are usually clipped and lower than they would be in standard English, so a double *a* is used to represent a longer a sound. In *bakwaas*, for example, the first syllable might equally be rendered in English as 'buk', while the second is longer than the first, more like the English word *was*. A *ch* is usually voiced slightly more than it would be in, say, *chop* – somewhere in between the standard English pronunciation of *ch* in *chop* and the *j* in *jury*. *Chh* (as in *chhokra*) is used to indicate that the *ch* is not voiced and is said as the soft *ch* in English. In *bh*, *gh*, and *dh*, there is the slightest hint of a *h*, as is sometimes heard in Scottish pronunciations of *what* or *where*. *B*s can be voiced like an English *v*, and *d*s like a harder English *th*, as is occasionally discernable in, for example, *that* when said in a mild Irish brogue.

aadat *noun* custom; habit

> well, it's all right once in a while; I hope he doesn't make it his aadat, that's all

aakar *noun* arrogance

> my friend says rich people can always afford to have aakar, but I disagree

aashique *noun* a male lover, especially one in a state of infatuation

> so there's this aashique and he's paagal over some rich little rani...

abba, abba-jaan *or* **abbu-jaan** *noun* father

> Abba-jaan, would you give me a lift to the station?

The word *abba* can be suffixed with *jaan* (Urdu for 'life') to convey greater affection on the part of the speaker.

ahimsa *noun* peacefulness; non-violence

> Gandhi defeated the British by relying on ahimsa, his doctrine of non-violence (*The Times*)

air-dash (in South Asia) | *verb* **1** to travel by air at short notice

> the Chief Minister air-dashed to the scene and ordered a CID probe into the disaster (*The Tribune*)

| *noun* **air dash** **2** an air journey undertaken at short notice

> London-based Pakistanis to make 'air dash' for Lahore marathon (*The Daily Times*)

aish *noun* pleasurable activity

> I just did aish at school. That's what happens when you've got old money behind you

akal *noun* common sense

> My son has no akal at all. If you told him to jump in a well he'd ask you which one

ammi *or* **ammi-jaan** *noun* mother

The word *ammi*, like *abba*, is often suffixed with *jaan* to convey affection on the part of the speaker.

> Ammi, could I have some more roti please?

andhar *adverb* inside

Bhai, it's going to rain, come andhar

Angrez *noun* an English person or English
people

> the Angrez might have gone but they left their children
> in government

Angrezi *adjective* **1** English

> Channel V is, finally, on its way to revamping its Angrezi
> image (*Business Today*)

| *noun* **2** the English language

> there's no point in having Asian dramas on telly if
> they're going to speak Angrezi all the time

anvil on the anvil (in South Asia) imminent; on
the agenda; slated to happen

> major amendments to Bill on the anvil (headline in *The
> Hindu*)

apna or (*feminine*) **apni** *noun, plural* **apne** a
person who belongs to the same community as
oneself

> Was that chap you met yesterday an apna?

apprehend *verb* (in South Asia) to await (something) with fear

> The police say that there is no evidence that links this family to the case. However, the girl's relatives have disappeared, apprehending police crackdown (*The Tribune*)

Although this sense of the word has fallen out of use in other forms of English around the world, it's still alive and well in India and Pakistan.

arre *interjection* an expression calling for another's attention

> Arre! Put that back!

asli *adjective* (in South Asia) real or genuine

> [MTV India] began by targeting a Gucci-sporting, Louis Vuitton-toting, Guns'N'Roses-doting audience. Then, they realised that these people barely existed. So they moved from American pie to dal makhani and from nasal drawls to asli desi accents, liberally peppered with Hindi (*The Hindu*)

Auntie-ji *noun* a name and a form of address

for any woman at least one generation older than oneself

> Just yesterday I had another auntie-ji pop round. She was speaking in hushed whispers but then again auntie-jis and hushed whispers don't really go hand in hand – I could hear every word upstairs

auto *noun informal* (in South Asia) an auto-rickshaw: a small three-wheeled motor vehicle used as a taxi, usually with a roof canopy and open sides

> he gazes out from the coffee parlour, where we're sitting, at the tangle of autos, scooters, cars, and buses trying to make headway on Bangalore's heaving CMH Road (*Business Today*)

babu *noun* **1** a form of address for any elderly man **2** *often derogatory* (in South Asia) a government official

> Who is a babu sitting in the Environment Ministry to decide on a particular animal or on the number of animals needed to test a vaccine? (*The Tribune*)

babudom *noun informal* (in South Asia)

1 bureaucracy as allegedly created and perpetuated by babus. *Also called* **babucracy 2** all babus considered collectively

> But instead of rightsizing babudom, the commission has come up with a solution typical of the babus. Instead of cutting back on the cost of governance, it intends to raise the Government's salary bill by 7,300 crore rupees (*India Today*)

bacha *or* (*feminine*) **bachi** *noun, plural* **bache** a child

> Have you got any bache of your own, then?

bachao *interjection* help (me)

> Bachao! Bachao! cries the damsel in distress in nearly every nineties flick you see. It's so pathetic

bada *adjective* big

> Our family has a name for the two Patel brothers' grocery stores; one is Bada Patel, and the other is Chota Patel. One store is like really big and grand-looking from the outside and the other is so small and dinky, but cheaper in price for the same products (from a blog on *Xanga.com*)

badmash *noun* **1** a hooligan; a thug; a dishonest person **2** *informal* a rascal

> that friend of yours is a good-for-nothing badmash

badmashi *noun* hooliganism; bad behaviour

> law and order is in an abysmal state with more dacoities, car snatchings, intimidation, extortion and general badmashi than ever before (*The International News*)

bahar *adverb* outside

> dad went bahar as soon as he heard auntie-ji was coming round

bakwaas *noun* spoken nonsense

> I hate to say it but some of your pedantic bakwaas really does my head in

balle-balle *interjection* **1** a joyous exclamation, used, for example, when a party is livening up | *verb* **2** to exclaim 'balle-balle'

> till even three years ago, Goa was the raver's heaven, the Ibiza-like space in a country that otherwise balle-balle-ed to bhangra and Bollywood remixes (*India Today*)

balti *noun* **a** a spicy Indian dish, stewed until most of the liquid has evaporated, and served in a wok-like pot **b** (*as modifier*): *a balti house*

> an ice-cold beer is an essential part of the British balti experience

The balti is a British Asian phenomenon. If you ask for a balti in India or Pakistan you are more likely to be handed a bucket, as it's the Urdu word for 'pail'. Initially used to describe the container this particular dish is cooked in, when used in Britain (where the dish was invented), the word now represents the curry itself.

bandar *or* (*feminine*) **bandari** *noun* **1** a monkey **2** *derogatory* a mischievous or impudent person

> Leave that alone, you little bandar!

bandh *noun* (in South Asia) a general strike

> police said stones were thrown at passing buses in some parts of the city where the bandh had evoked

a fair response with shops and other commercial establishments closed (*Samāchar*)

bandobust *noun* protection, esp that provided by police or other security services at polling stations during elections

> It should be possible for it to declare the results if not the same evening at least the next day. The logistics of security and other bandobust cannot be an excuse for keeping the people in a state of suspended animation (*NewIndPress.com*)

bas *interjection* enough

> Bas! I can't bear to hear you spout that rubbish any longer

batameez *adjective* bad-mannered

> no wonder he's batameez, the way you treat him

batchmate *noun* (in South Asia) a person who is or was enrolled in one's year at school, on a course, etc, but not necessarily in the same class

> not surprisingly, the internet is littered with alumni associations, batchmate networks and league listings (*India Today*)

bechara *or* (*feminine*) **bechari** *noun* an unfortunate person

>he's lost everything – the poor bechara never had a
>chance, really

behn *noun* sister > *See* **Family Ties, page 50**

bela *or* **vela,** (*feminine*) **beli** *or* **veli** *adjective* unemployed; inactive

>It's no wonder Sanju is still bela. He hasn't even
>bothered to apply for a job since April

berth *noun* (in South Asia) a seat in government

>A defeat will rob him of the prestige he has enjoyed all
>his life. And a win may see him through to a berth in the
>Union Cabinet (*India Today*)

besharm *noun* a shameless person

>the women at the mandir said that Nina was such a
>besharm because she came in showing her midriff

besharmi *noun* shamelessness

>it's the height of besharmi to do that among friends
>never mind in a public place

Fashion

It wasn't very long ago that, for South Asian women in the UK, the need for a new *salwar kameez* meant buying a length of seersucker fabric off a fabric roll, hitting the sewing machine, and hoping for the best. Even less convenient (and much more expensive) was buying a *sari*, which meant a return ticket to the sub-continent instead of the local fashion store.

Thankfully, this has all changed in the last decade: South Asian fashion in all its varying forms has moved into the high street and is, it seems, here to stay. That a few celebrities have sported the odd *bindi* has helped, as has the West's blossoming love affair with the glitz, the glamour, and the beauty of Bollywood. The richness of colour and fabric of the *sherwani* and the bridal *lehanga* worn at Asian weddings seems to have been the inspiration behind many designs, with the intricate embroidery now appearing on kaftans and shirts on the high street. Embroidered *khusse* and *chappal* can be found almost everywhere, and are worn with jeans to add colour and sparkle, and Boho chic has embraced the *bangle.*

besti *noun* shame or embarrassment, especially that experienced after a joke has been played at one's expense, or when one has done something foolish

> so there you are on your stag night, completely naked, and out come the camera phones to broadcast your besti far and wide

beta *noun* **1** son **2** an affectionate term of address for any young boy

> Davinder beta, are you not hungry?

beti *noun* **1** daughter **2** an affectionate term of address for any young girl

> Beti Sadiya, where is your massi today?

bevakoof *or* **befkoof** *noun* a fool

> Honestly, that boy is such a bevakoof. He shouldn't be allowed out in public

bevakoofi *or* **befkoofi** *noun* foolishness

> it is complete bevakoofi to trust the newspapers these days

bhabi *noun* the wife of one's brother > *see* **Family Ties, page 50**

bhai *or* **bhaiya** *noun* *informal* **1** (a form of address for) a man one considers as a brother, whether related by blood or not

> Hey bhai, will you give me a lift to work? My car's at the garage

2 (in Mumbai) a slang term for a gangster boss; a don

> Raju comes up with yet another plan to rob neighbouring wannabe bhai (Johnny Lever) of a few crores worth of heroin (*BollywoodWorld.com*)

bhaji *noun* *informal* (a form of address for) a woman one considers as a sister, whether related by blood or not

> I saw bhaji in the market again, hunting for the latest fabric as usual

bhangra *noun* a type of Asian pop music and

dance that combines elements of traditional Punjabi music with Western pop

> her sound is an explosive mix of bhangra, ragga, electro and hip-hop (*The Times*)

bidi *noun* a thin home-made cigarette of tobacco rolled up in a tendu (East Indian ebony) leaf

> The clan being rather dipsomaniacal, as the night sets in, almost everybody – wives, sons, granddaughters-in-law – hits the bottle. It is not uncommon to see Patti, already high on the local brew, smoking a bidi (*India Today*)

bindaas *adjective* cool, carefree

> Bombay's bindaas college-going chhokras and chhokris

> That rave was pure bindaas! Never seen so many people jamming like that

bindi *or* **bindhi** *noun* a decorative marking traditionally worn by married Hindu women in the middle of the forehead

> She sports bindis on her collarbone or at the corners of her eyes – any place except where you are supposed to! (*India Today*)

Bindis were traditionally worn by married Hindu women and taken as an indicator of their married status. They were applied to the forehead as this is an important *chakra* – centre of energy – in Hindu belief. These days, however, the bindi is increasingly worn as a fashion statement, by women of all ages, and on parts of the body other than the forehead. The designs of the bindis themselves are changing and can take the form of triangles or even vertical lines of any colour.

biwi *noun* wife

> his biwi is his biggest fan

Bollywood *noun* *informal* **1** the Indian film industry **2** the imaginary world portrayed in Bollywood films **3** (*as modifier*): *a Bollywood star*

> Channel 4's search for a home-grown Bollywood star received 1,000 applications from hopefuls (*The Sunday Times*)

This seemingly innocuous term has raised hackles in some quarters, and on a couple of points. Firstly, the word *Bollywood* was coined in reference to films produced in the city of Mumbai (it's a blend of *Bombay* – Mumbai's former name – and *Hollywood*). These days, the term is used as a catchall for all Indian films, regardless of where they were made, and some feel this does a disservice to India's other centres of film production. A second objection is that the name implies that the Indian film industry is a merely an imitation of the 'real' American version, when in fact the two traditions are very different, and India produces many more movies than the US.

buda *or (feminine)* **budi** *noun derogatory* an old person

> he might look young but he's just a buda on the inside

bustee *noun* (in India and Bangladesh) a slum or shanty town

> *City of Joy* is set in the sprawling bustees of Calcutta, the world's largest concentration of slums in what's been called the world's most afflicted and extraordinary city (*National Public Radio*)

carrying *adjective* (in India) pregnant

> I'm sure his wife is carrying again but he's not said anything about it yet

chacha *or* **chachu** *noun* one's father's younger brother > *See* **Family Ties, page 50**

chachi *noun* the wife of one's father's younger brother > *See* **Family Ties, page 50**

chai tea > *see* **masala chai**

> all this chai is boiled with condensed milk, cardamom and sugar: it is thick, sweet and spicy – an Indian cuppa (*Country Living*)

chai-paani *noun* **1** food and drink

> You are a guest in our home. I insist you have some chai-paani. I will not take no for an answer

2 *euphemistic* (in South Asia) tips or bribes paid to get (for example) speedier processing of applications; low-level corruption

> in fact, chai paani corruption may not have major negative consequences for economic growth (*The Daily Times*)

chak de phatte *interjection informal* an exhortation to be joyful, often exclaimed at parties and clubs

> bhangra is most probably the closest thing India has to dance music and, despite its reputation for livening up a party with its trademark 'chak de phatte' slogan...its lyrics are often rooted in gritty social realism reflecting life in Punjabi communities (*The Guardian*)

There are many theories as to how this expression came about. The phrase literally means 'pick up the planks'. Some espouse the notion that it is encouraging all present to dance with such vigour that the floorboards are ripped up, reminiscent of established English idioms such as 'bring

the house down' and 'raise the roof'. Other
more convoluted explanations include the
suggestion that it is an ancient war cry
once yelled by Sikh raiders returning from
a successful sortie, urging the hindmost
to tear up the makeshift bridges they had
built not long before to invade enemy
territory, thus preventing pursuit. Whatever
its origins, it's fairly clear that if you hear
it these days you know you're in the right
place.

chakka *noun* (*in cricket*) a six

> I'll never forget the chakka I scored in the last over of
> the final

chalaak *adjective* sly; crafty; artful

> You need to watch out for that one. She's very chalaak

chaliye *interjection* let's go; shall we go?

> Come on, get up. Chaliye!

chalta hai *phrase* **1 a** it will suffice; it will do **b** anything goes! **2** (*as modifier*): *chalta-hai attitude*

> Our age-old chalta-hai attitude will have to be entirely dispensed with. Many organisations are ridden with the malaise of excuses for non-performance (*Business Today*)

In Hindi the phrase *chalta hai* literally means 'it goes' and is often used as shorthand for a certain careless approach to life and flexible attitude to rules which many Indians think characterizes their country's collec tive psyche. Opinion there is sharply divided as to whether this supposed 'chalta hai' mindset is a charming idiosyncracy that makes India the diverse and exciting place it is, or a cultural millstone that keeps the nation from performing to its potential on the world stage.

chamcha *noun* **1** a spoon **2** *informal* (in India) **a** a lackey **b** an obsequious person; a sycophant

> chamchas are like roaches, able to survive in any nook and corner – from petty offices to the power corridors of Parliament (letter in *The Hindu*)

The origins of the second sense of the word are uncertain. While there are several suggestions as to why the Hindi word for 'spoon' has become synonymous with an obsequious person, the most convincing is that it comes from the notion, once widely held in South Asia, that native South Asians who used cutlery to eat were merely trying to ingratiate themselves with Westerners by imitating their habits.

chamchagiri *noun* sycophancy

> Chamchagiri is hard work. To do it well, one really needs an aptitude for this kind of thing (*BusinessworldIndia. com*)

changa *interjection informal* an expression of approval; okay, all right, etc

> Changa, then – let's go

chappal *noun* an item of footwear resembling a flip-flop, often with a loop that goes around the big toe

> Unwashed jeans, tousled hair, and rubber chappals. This seems to be the uniform of the students of the Indian Institute of Science in Bangalore (*Business Today*)

> don't worry, I don't engage in chappal-throwing; I'm not that sort of feminist (*Pickled Politics*)

Chappals are often brandished and thrown in India when protests get out of hand, so often in fact that the 'chappal-throwing' demonstrator has become something of an Indian political stereotype. This ballistic application of slippers is largely due to two factors: symbolically, they are seen as unclean, adding insult to slight risk of injury, and practically, they can be taken off and launched in the blink of an eye.

chargesheet *verb* (in South Asia) to press criminal

charges against (someone)

> but once he is chargesheeted, the people could well turn their backs on him – as has happened with so many seasoned politicians in the recent past (*India Today*)

char-sau-bees *noun* *informal* (in India) a fraudster or con artist

> they say he's a char-sau-bees and a womanizer

Char-sau-bees is Hindi for the number 420, which corresponds to the section of the Indian penal code relating to fraud.

char-sau-beesi *noun* fraud or cheating

> I swear there's more char-sau-beesi from that girl every year!

chawal, chawl *or* **chaval** *noun* rice

> I have simple tastes; dal, roti, and chawal are enough for me

chhokra *or* (*feminine*) **chhokri** *noun* a youth; a youngster

> Bombay's bindaas school and college-going chhokras

and chhokris (*Outlook India*)

chi-chi *interjection* *informal* an expression of disapproval or even disgust; yuck!

> Did you see the way she eats her food? Chi-chi, it's so unladylike!

choli *noun* a blouse that is cut off at the midriff, often worn with a **sari** or a **lehenga**

> only the sartorially inept will team a sari with a choli that does not quite match the ground colour or echo one of the tints in the borders or motifs (*The Times*)

chor *noun, plural* **chor** a thief

> Why is it that the police never seem to catch these chor?

chota *adjective* small

> he's so chota I doubt anyone will go out with him

chowk *noun* (in South Asia) a market place

> special facilities for purchasing Rajasthani handicrafts, jewellery and art and fashion products will be developed at the chowk (*The Hindu*)

chuddies *plural noun* *informal* underpants

> Why don't they make sexy designer chuddies for men, like thongs, where women get to see men's butts in full view? (*Sulekha.com Forum*)

The word *chuddies* was introduced into the mainstream British vocabulary in the 1990s by the BBC comedy show *Goodness Gracious Me!*, and in particular by the catchphrase 'Kiss my chuddies, man!'

chugliyan *noun* gossip; chat

> in my opinion men are as bad as women when it comes to chugliyan

cinema *noun* (in India) a film

> that was the best cinema I've seen all year

colony *noun* (in India) an apartment complex

> the girl's family lives in a colony on the Pakhowal Road (*The Tribune*)

countrymade *adjective* (in South Asia) (of offically regulated commodities such as alcohol and firearms) made illegally

Patna police today busted off an illegal arms factory today following a tip-off and took four people into custody. Large numbers of countrymade arms were recovered in the raid (*OnlyPunjab.com*)

cousin brother *noun* (in South Asia) a male cousin

> you should see my cousin brother's car

cousin sister *noun* (in South Asia) a female cousin

> I'm going to stay with my cousin sister in Delhi

crore *noun* a unit equal to 10 million > *Compare* **lakh**

> unfortunately facts are totally different as the state is heading towards a debt trap with an overall debt running into almost one lakh crores of rupees (*Samachar*)

crorepati *noun* a person who has assets worth at least one crore rupees

> Infosys, the darling of the capital markets for nearly a decade, is credited with the creation of a legion of

crorepatis (*The Hindu Business Line*)

cutting chai *noun* (in Mumbai) a half measure of chai, as sold by the roadside > *see entries for* **chai, masala chai**

> In Mumbai, if you want to get half a glass of hot tea from your friendly roadside establishment, you ask for a 'cutting chai'. This is the usual serving size. If you're radical enough to want a whole glass, it's a 'double cutting chai'. And we supposedly invented math (a post on the blog *What's New, Pussycat?*)

daada *noun* one's paternal grandfather > *See* **Family Ties, page 50**

daadi *noun* one's paternal grandmother > *See* **Family Ties, page 50**

dabba *noun* a box (especially a lunchbox)

> Vrinda Bhalekar hands over an aluminium container with piping hot lunch for her husband to a middle-aged man wearing the regulation white cap. In an hour's time, the man will have collected 30 such dabbas (lunch boxes) to pass on to a waiting colleague at the local railway station (*India Today*)

dabbawallah *noun* (in Mumbai) a dabba delivery man

> behind the reliable-as-clockwork system is a relay of thousands of hardworking dabbawallahs and a simple but effective coding system (*India Today*)

The delivery system perfected by the dabbawallahs of Mumbai is a minor miracle of logistics. Every day 4,500 of them collect some 160,000 dabbas from workers' homes, and bring them to a sorting office where the tin boxes are relayed to the relevant workplace. When the grateful recipients have eaten the contents, the process is reversed and the dabbas are brought back through the sorting office and returned to the people (usually wives or mothers) who prepared them a few hours previously. The dabbawallahs use all manner of transport – hand-drawn carts, bicycles, trains, etc – and

keep track of the destination and provenance of each dabba by referring to a painted code on its lid. Although the majority of the dabbawallahs are illiterate, the relay system is held up by business analysts as a world-class model of efficient distribution. *Forbes Magazine* recently awarded the dabbawallahs a rating of 6 Sigma, which equates to one dabba going astray in every 6 million transactions!

dacoity *noun* robbery; banditry

> alarmed by the spate of dacoities, jewellers are opting for state-of-the-art security systems for their showrooms (*India Today*)

dai *noun, plural* **dai** (in South Asia) a midwife

> in the Tansa Region, 89.5 percent of births are attended by untrained dai who do not always immediately recognize emergency situations, who may perform deliveries under unhygienic conditions, and who do not have access to adequate emergency transportation (*www.prasad.org*)

dandian *noun* a traditional Gujarati dance in which dancers hold decorated sticks (**dandias**)

> Ever heard of dandian? The dance? You must have seen it on TV or the movies. Well, at the festival you do that dance, it's fun

desi *informal* | *adjective* **1** authentically South Asian

> in an era of muscled boy-toys and westernised star sons, he [Govinda] is an authentic desi delight (*India Today*)

| *noun* **2** a person considered to be authentically South Asian

> Most desis had either black, blue or silver Beemers, but Ravi's was a purply kind of metallic grey (*Londonstani* by Gautam Malkani)

dharna *noun* (in South Asia) a protest, often combined with a fast, in which demonstrators stand outside an establishment for an extended period

> a group of lawyers went on dharna in front of the high court in Chennai for three days last week (*India Today*)

dhikkar *noun* (in India) **1** an expression of condemnation **2** *(as modifier)*: *a dhikkar rally*

> The word *dhikkar* is not easy to translate. It is a jumble of an expletive, a curse, a nasty exclamation…For an effective *dhikkar*, one would have to register a grimace (*The Indian Express*)

dhol *noun* a large barrel-shaped drum which is beaten at times of celebration, often in accompaniment to bhangra

> the melody is rather hidden under the thumping dhol beat on this track

didi *noun* *informal* (one's) sister > *See* **Family Ties, page 50**

dishum-dishum *noun* *informal* **a** the scenes in Bollywood films that depict stylized fist fights **b** *as modifier*: *dishum-dishum films*

> very predictable with the inevitable 'dishum-dishum' at the end, but still an enjoyable flick

doosra *adjective* **1** second | *noun* **2** *cricket* a delivery, bowled by an off-spinner, that turns the opposite way from an off-break, i.e., it turns from the batsman's leg side towards the side of the field to which he presents his bat

you need to take the doosra turn on the left

The cricketing doosra was invented in the 1990s by Pakistan international Saqlain Mushtaq. Up until then no off-spinner (a bowler who specializes in making the ball turn from a right-handed batsman's right-hand – or 'off' – side to his left-hand – or 'leg' – side) had managed to make the ball turn in this way. The delivery got its name because whenever the Pakistani wicket keeper judged the situation ripe for Mushtaq to bowl his secret weapon he would call out 'doosra', meaning 'the second one', the second delivery in his repertoire.

dosti *noun* (in South Asia) friendship; good relations

> Do you think Punjabi dosti could hold the key to better relations between the two countries? The two Punjabs have a lot in common with each other (*Outlook India*)

dupatta *noun* a type of Indian scarf

> they wore plastic slippers and were draped in flowing, brilliantly coloured dupattas and skirts with coins sewn into them (*The Carpet Wars* by C Kremmer)

eve-teasing *noun* *informal* (in South Asia) the sexual harassment of women and girls, especially in public

> Every action is performed with an intention. The intention behind eve-teasing is: to catch a girl's eye and to arouse attention in some way; and more importantly this harassment is an early manifestation of patriarchal masculinity (*The Hindu*)

faltoo *noun* useless

> all these electronic gizmos my son buys for me are faltoo

fikar *verb* to worry fikar not don't worry

I'm going to miss all of you but fikar not; I shall return!

filmi *informal* | *adjective* **1** melodramatic; reminiscent of or suitable for a typical Indian film

> You should have seen cousin Bela's wedding. It was very filmi; that's all I'm going to say!

2 of or relating to film or the film industry

> this is all I've ever known, being from a filmi family where everybody has been into acting and direction (*India Today*)

| *noun* **3** music written and performed specifically for Indian cinema

> Till but a few years ago, there were three distinct genres in music. They were the classical, the western pop and the filmi. And the three never quite mingled (*India Today*)

firang *adjective* (in India) foreign

> Call centres to stop faking 'firang' accent. Call centre executives can at last throw their Texas drawls or fancy Brit inflections out of the window. BPOs (Business Process Outsourcing companies) have decided to do away with foreign accents in favour of plain, natural

English (*Sify.com*)

firangi *noun* a foreigner

> Of course, firangis have always been part of the Indian
> outsourcing scene. But until recently, they were mostly
> highly paid experts from companies that were sending
> their work abroad, helping the new Indian team learn
> the processes (*BusinessWeek*)

Firang and *firangi* (or *feringhee*) derive
ultimately from 'Frank', via the Arabic *al-
faranji*. This reflects the designation of all
Roman Catholic Europeans as 'Franks' by
the Arabs in the Middle Ages. The Thai term
farang has the same origin.

fob *informal, derogatory* *acronym for* 'fresh off
the boat': a recent immigrant, especially one
considered to be be stereotypically South Asian in
his or her appearance or outlook > fobby *adjective*

> well, I'm technically not a fob, but that doesn't stop
> me from talking in a fobby desi accent all day long
> sometimes

freshie *noun informal, derogatory* a recent immigrant: short for 'fresh off the boat'

> All the freshies would be lining up outside the embassy trying to get a British visa

fundas *plural noun informal* (in India) fundamentals; basics

> I've just been talking to my stockbroker, but it feels like I went to a shrink. Instead of investment counselling, the guy is trying to change all my fundas on investing (*Business Today*)

gaddi *noun* **1** a type of cushion

> and the most common sight [in a wholesalers] even today is the babu sitting on a gaddi juggling three telephones and sundry suppliers (*Business Today*)

2 (in India) *informal* an official position, esp one in government

> The office of prime minister has been exposed to ridicule and mirth, thanks to the nomination of a non-leader to keep the chair warm till another Indian-born member of the Nehru-Gandhi dynasty feels confident enough to acquire the family 'gaddi' (*Samachar*)

gandh *noun* vulgarity; smut; filth (literally 'odour')

> there's too much gandh in films these days

gandha or (*feminine*) **gandhi** *adjective* vulgar; smutty; filthy

> I couldn't even watch the male lead dancing, he was so gandha

ganja *adjective* **1** having no hair on the head; bald

> Dad's gone all ganja since he's started working at the bank

2 lacking natural covering

> Pakistan begin their tour game on a ganja wicket

garam *adjective* hot; spicy

> chai's not chai if it isn't garam

gar-barh *noun* *informal* trouble; violence

> there was a lot of gar-barh after the match yesterday

gharwali *noun* (in South Asia) **1** a housewife

> The woman [who I've been chatting up] drives off with

my leather jacket. Just don't tell my gharwali! (forum on *gupshup.com*)

2 a female brothel keeper; a madam

> [the area] housed 23 bars in a 25,000 sq metre area, and 100 'gharwalis' who kept a tight leash on the business through a network of pimps and cops on the pay, a project worker said (*The Deccan Herald*)

ghazal *noun* **1** a type of love poem consisting, in its simplest form, of a collection of two-line stanzas **2** a musical rendering of this sort of love lyric

> Abida's lilting ghazals, sung with tremendous verve and vigour, went on past midnight, with 300 pairs of hands clapping along in sheer ecstasy

giddha *noun* a vigorous Punjabi folk dance performed by women and characterized by intricate rhythmic clapping

> women have a different but no less exuberant dance called giddha

glassy *noun* *informal* a glass of alcoholic drink

I fancy a glassy or two tonight

gobar gas *noun* (in South Asia) a type of fuel in the form of methane gas derived from manure

> If you are the green type, the solar water heaters, low-energy lamps, and gobar gas plants within the premises should warm the cockles of your activist heart (*Business Today*)

godown *noun* (in South Asia) a warehouse

> last month, a former construction goods godown was fitted out with beds and mattresses to accommodate 30 students, three to a room (*India Today*)

gora *or* (*feminine*) **gori** *noun, plural* **gore** *or* **goras,** (*feminine*) **gore** *or* **goris a** a white person **b** a person with fair skin

> I [DJ Markie Mark] was raised in a desi neighbourhood, always hung around with the desi crowd. So I have always had the Asian crew behind me, they know where I'm coming from even though I'm a gora (*Desi Tunes 4 U*)

> as for us goris in desi clothes, I think that most times we just don't have a feel for it, what looks right colourwise and cutwise…(*conversation*)

Gujju *informal, sometimes used derogatively*
1 *noun* a Gujurati person (i.e. a member of a
people of India living chiefly in Gujurat) |
adjective **2** Gujurati: *Gujju food*

> where there are Gujjus, there is antakshari

gunda *noun, plural* **gunde** *or* **gundas** *derogatory*
a hooligan; a man who behaves in a violent or
uncouth manner

> There's gunde loitering on every corner

In South Asia the term means 'gangster', but
in Britain it is generally used to indicate a
less serious level of criminality.

gup-shup *noun* *informal* a chat; get-together;
chit-chat

> I've asked Chachi to come round our house for some
> samose and a gup-shup

gurdwara *noun* a Sikh place of worship

> entering the vast gurdwara, we took off our shoes and
> covered our heads and then traversed a hall as big as a

country on a narrow strip of red carpet to bow before the Sri Guru Granth, a holy text (*The Times*)

The word *gurdwara* ultimately comes from Sanskrit meaning 'teacher's (guru's) door'.

gyan *noun* knowledge or understanding; wisdom

it's December and hey, it's Monday morning and is there any better way to start a whole new week than with the one and only Gyan Guru wakin' you guys up with all the gyan in town? (*The Hindu*)

haan *sentence substitute* yes

'Feeling better today?' 'Haan'

hafta *noun* (in India) a bribe

One unauthorised bookseller from West Bengal, says he has to be ready to run at a moment's notice. If caught, the city authority seizes his books in the morning and then returns them in the evening if the hafta is paid, he said (*The Guardian*)

haina *question tag* isn't it?

Amitabh Bachan is the best, haina?

In Hindi *haina* means literally 'is-no'. It is

used at the end of a sentence to ascertain if someone is listening or in agreement. This construction has undoubtedly contributed to the popularity of the similar tag *innit* that crops up continually in British urban dialect, irrespective of grammatical aptness ('because I want to, innit'). Although, strictly, *innit?* should be a straight swap only for 'isn't it?', it's actually used (like *haina*) to stand in for a variety of different questions (*Isn't it, won't I, don't they, can't I, do you*, etc).

haramzada *or* **haramda,** (*feminine*) **haramzadi** *or* **haramdi** *noun offensive slang* **1** a person born of unmarried parents **2** an obnoxious or despicable person

> He stood aghast for a while and, on regaining his wits, he said, "I ought to have known better than trust a haramzada like you!" (*Tales of Boyd* by S.D. Banerjea)

Family ties

Every member of a South Asian family has a specific title, and an abundance of terms is necessary to describe those members of the extended family who live both within the household and in the wider community.

The average attendance of an Asian wedding (in excess of three hundred) demonstrates the concept of family for the British Asian community, where 'family' can mean those with whom there may be historical or geographical ties. The terms *Uncle Ji* and *Auntie Ji* are applied to a person who is not a blood relation. *Ji* is used to convey respect, usually towards a person at least a generation older than oneself.

In a family you can call:

- your sister *behn* (or more informally *didi*), and her husband *jija*
- your brother's wife *bhabi*
- your mother's father *nana* and your mother's mother *nani*; your mother's younger brother *mama* or *mamu* and his wife *mami*; your mother's elder sister *massi* and her husband *massar*
- your father's father *daada* and your father's mother *daadi*; your father's younger brother *chacha* or *chachu* and his wife *chachi*; your father's elder sister *pua* (in Urdu *pupi*) and her husband *phuphar* (in Urdu *pupr*); your father's elder brother *thaiya* and his wife *thaiyee*
- your wife's brother *sala* and your wife's sister *sali*

hatke *adjective* quirky; off-beat; departing from convention

> Actors always sound so clichéd when they say their film is a little hatke. It is obvious that they are acting in another stale melodrama

hauli *adjective* **haulier, hauliest** **1** slow | *adverb* **2** slowly

> Go a bit haulier, you lunatic!

hawala *noun* (in South Asia) an illegal system for the transfer of funds between one place and another, especially from western countries into India or Pakistan

> One reason [for using hawala] is efficiency. A hawala remittance takes place in, at most, one or two days. (*Interpol's website*)

Hawala is an ancient system that allows users to move money across huge distances. Or rather to move credit, for the cash itself doesn't travel. It was developed at least 1200 years ago, when moving large amounts

of currency along the Silk Road or across
the seas was a much more difficult and
risky business than it is now. Reduced to
its most basic form, modern hawala works
like this: if I want to send some money, say
to my cousin in Delhi, I take my cash to a
hawaladar. He calls one of his associates in
Delhi, gives him my cousin's details, and asks
him to pay the equivalent amount in rupees,
less a commission competitive enough
to undercut official exchange rates. The
hawaladar at my end then settles the debt
with his Delhi counterpart at a later date.
It's a huge network relying on trust. Little
or no paperwork is kept about individual
transactions, so it is easy for the hawaladars
and their clients to avoid legal repercussions.

hawaladar *noun* (in South Asia) a hawala broker

the fees charged by hawaladars on the transfer of

funds are lower than those charged by banks and other remitting companies, thanks mainly to minimal overhead expenses and the absence of regulatory costs to the hawaladars, who often operate other small businesses (*Finance & Development*)

heat and dust *noun* (in India) upheaval or turmoil

in the heat and dust that this single issue generates, other issues are conveniently forgotten (*Outlook India*)

hera-pheri *noun* unscrupulous, improper, or illegal dealings

I tell you what, there was a lot of hera-pheri going on at our poker night last weekend

Hinglish *noun informal* **a** (in Britain) the use of certain words from a South Asian language, esp Hindi, Urdu, or Punjabi in a predominantly English spoken sentence **b** (in India) the use of English words in a predominantly Hindi, Urdu, or Punjabi spoken sentence

Hinglish, the hybrid of Hindi and English spoken as a second language by 350 million Indians, may soon become the most common spoken form of English,

British linguist David Crystal told *The Times* (*The Times*)

history-sheeter *noun* (in South Asia) a person with a lengthy criminal record

> just last week, a controversial character and history-sheeter won the elections to the state Legislative Council on a BJP ticket (*India Today*)

horn OK please (in India) a phrase painted on the back of commercial vehicles requesting that drivers of overtaking vehicles sound their horns before passing

> India's anarchy was in full swing, buses saying, 'Silence please' on their sides, the mudguards of trucks responding with 'Horn OK please' (*Prospect Magazine*)

hungama *noun* (in India) a commotion; a stir

> since [they both] had worn skimpy clothes their dance show created a hungama all over the city (*Indian Inside*)

Indipop *noun* *informal* (in India) Indian pop music

> English translations of 18th-century Sufi poet Bulla Shah's words seem unlikely on a chart-topping Indipop

debut album sleeve. But then, everything about Rabbi Shergill is unlikely (*Rediff.com*)

intimate *verb* (in South Asia) to make (someone) aware; to notify (someone)

> the Committee is overwhelmed with thousands of applications every year, so please do not call to find out – you will be intimated if you are through to the next stage (*RhodesIndia.com*)

izzat *noun* honour or sense of respect

> How can I insult her izzat when she had none in the first place?

jaan *noun* **1** life **2** a term of endearment for someone whom one feels is an important part of one's life

> he's my jaan and I love him to bits

jaldi-jaldi *interjection* *informal* an exhortation to go faster

> Why are you taking so long? Come on, jaldi-jaldi!

jalebi *noun* **1** a pretzel-shaped sweet

a jalebi, by the way, is molten sugar charmed by a fakir
into the shape of a Curly Wurly and served in a paper
bag (*The Times*)

2 a a beloved or lovable person **b** a term of
endearment for such a person

Big dreamy eyes and a beautiful smile – two more
reasons why my jalebi makes me melt

javaan *or* **jawan** *adjective* in the prime of one's
youth

I'm far too javaan to think about getting hitched

javaani *or* **jawani** *noun* youth

My mum used to wear tight clothes in her javaani

jhatka *noun* **1 a** the traditional Sikh method of
slaughtering livestock humanely and without
religious ritual, using only one blow so that death
occurs quickly **b** (*as modifier*): *jhatka meat*

a Sikh's lifestyle must also be characterised by purity
– avoiding tobacco, alcohol and other intoxicants and
eating only 'jhatka' meat (*London Metropolitan University
website*)

| *adjective* **2** (in India) *informal* (of a Bollywood song-and-dance routine) featuring a lot of pelvic gyrations

> Mithun [Chakraborty], after what seemed like a sabbatical from his inimitable jhatka numbers and dishum-dishum flicks, is poised to grace the silver screen once more (*IndiaPlaza.com*)

The second sense of *jhatka* is derived from the first, following logic laced with gallows humour. When animals are dispatched by the jhatka method they often sway back and forth for a few seconds before falling over. Hardly a flattering comparison, but one that makes sense in a macabre sort of way, as well as illustrating the lack of squeamishness with which South Asians approach life – and death.

jija *noun* the husband of one's sister > *See* **Family Ties, page 50**

jollu party *noun informal* (in India) a lecherous person

> he's such a clown. A real jollu party – he drools at everything in a skirt (*blogger.com*)

jooth *noun* (in Sikh custom) food contaminated by the touch of another living creature

> my friend is a strict Sikh so she can't eat any jooth

josh *noun* (in South Asia) passion; zest; enthusiasm

> Having watched on TV the dare-devil acrobatics of the [Indian Air Force pilots] the students were an inspired lot, full of 'josh' to get acquainted with the life, training and professionalism of this mighty force (*The Tribune*)

kaajal *noun* a cosmetic made from sulphide and used like an eyeliner

> Sammy, on her part, was wearing a small nose ring, lots of kaajal around her eyes, and kept stylishly shaking her head to throw her hair back (*India Currents*)

kaala *or* (*feminine*) **kaali** *noun* 1 the colour black 2 *sometimes offensive* a Black person | *adjective*

3 black

> check out that kaali, she's hot

kameez *noun* a long loose-fitting shirt worn by both men and women, often worn with **shalwar**

> Katherine Hammett who, for many, produced the best show in Milan, mixed very crumpled western linen suits with knee-length kameez shirts (*Esquire8*)

kamina *or (feminine)* **kamini** *noun derogatory* a wretch; a contemptible person

> Hey, that kamini stole my purse!

kamla *or (feminine)* **kamli** *noun* a silly person

> I'm a complete kamli whenever he's around

kasme *interjection* I swear!

> It wasn't me, kasme!

kaura *or* **kauri** *adjective* (of food, spices, etc) causing a burning sensation in the mouth; hot and spicy

> Ammi, the dhal is too kauri again

The very first Indian restaurant in the UK was
the Hindostanee Coffee House in Portman
Square, London, which was opened in 1773 by
Sake Dean Mahomet from Patna. It wasn't until
the early twentieth century, however, that the
phenomenon of the 'Indian' restaurant or curry
house, as we know it today, really took off. The
earliest South Asian restaurant kitchens worked
with a one-pot system, where a *thurka* (sauce) was
made as a base for creating dishes such as the
korma and *jalfrezi*.

There are now over eight thousand
restaurants in Britain serving their own version
of South Asian regional cuisine, and it should
come as no surprise that, over time, food has
been adapted for the British palate. Dishes such
as the ever-popular *masala* are very much British

Asian creations, and it's unlikely that they would ever be served at any table in India or Pakistan. It's a rare thing indeed to hear a child of South Asian descent say "My Mum cooked a great vindaloo last night!"

Even dishes widely regarded in the UK as 'truly authentic' are anglicized, such as the *balti*, an anglicized form of the Urdu word meaning 'bucket'. The balti is thought to have been popularized in the 'Balti Belt' of Sparkhill and Sparkbrook in Birmingham, where restaurants cooked huge amounts of curries in big buckets.

In the last few years there has been a backlash against the anglicization of South Asian food, with *dhosas* (thin Indian pancakes made with gram flower) and *lassi* cropping up on menus UK-wide.

Why is it that when men go to a restaurant they have to order the most kaura dish on the menu?

kee-a *sentence substitute* a phrase meaning 'what is it?'

You bought me a present? Kee-a?

khalas (chiefly in Mumbai) *informal* | *adjective*
1 done; finished; complete | *interjection*
2 enough; no more!

I usually do about two hours of study when I come home, then I'm khalas

Khalas then! It's over. I'm sick of making your dinner and then doing all the dishes every night.

khusse *plural noun* flat usually embroidered slip-on shoes

nowadays everyone wears their khusse with their jeans

kidaah *sentence substitute* *informal* how are you?

Kidaah? Haven't seen you for ages

Pop culture

The British South Asian community is no longer
reliant on films and soap operas imported
from *Bollywood* (now a billion dollar industry
producing around 800 titles a year), *Lollywood* (its
Pakistani counterpart), and *Tollywood* (the Teluga
language film industry).

Traditional South Asian viewing habits
are still catered for, with satellite, cable, and
digital channels such as *Sony*, *B4U*, *Alpha*, and *Zee*
showing soaps that portray the dramas of affluent
Asian households, as well as music channels
with voluptuous 'item girls' performing 'item
numbers': songs from films that have little to do
with the narrative.

When it comes to films and theatre,
British Asian output has grown massively
in terms of both ambition and success over

the past decade, with popular and critically-acclaimed films such as *Bhaji on the Beach*, *Bend it like Beckham*, and *Anita and Me* all being produced in the UK. London's West End is more glamorous than ever, with *Bombay Dreams* running since 2002, and 2006 seeing the UK tour of the *Merchants of Bollywood*. Those more interested in dance than song can always turn to choreographer Akram Khan, whose cross-disciplinary collaborations are feted the world over.

Throughout the sixties and seventies, whenever Asian music was mentioned in a global context, the great Ravi Shankar would instantly leap to mind. These days a plethora of other artists and genres are jostling with the great man for air-time. Roots remain strong, though, from the Bhangra sensation that began in the mid-1980s, through Talvin Singh, Nitin Sawhney, and

Transglobal Underground to Richi-Rich's mix of authentic, traditional Asian music, hip-hop beats, smooth R 'n' B, and mainstream pop, and Swami's *Desi Rock*.

While modern Indian English literature is celebrated: Arundhati Roy's Booker Prize-winning *The God of Small Things*, the works of Vikram Seth, Anita Desai, and R. K. Narayan to name but a few, British Asian literature is enjoying a purple patch. Hanif Kureshi's *Buddha of Suburbia*, Monica Ali's *Brick Lane*, and *Londonstani* by Gautam Malkani are just three of many British Asian novels that have made their mark on the literary world.

kissa *noun* (in India) a story

> kissa kiss ka: new tech prises open cell of privacy (*The Times of India*)

The quotation is a headline from an article about an offscreen kiss between two celebrities being caught on a camera phone and broadcast on the internet. 'Kissa (something) ka' means 'the story of (something)'.

kitty party *noun* (in South Asia) a gathering of women who meet regularly to host sweepstakes and exchange gossip

> Everybody who is anybody in this megacity of 25 lakh is a member of one kitty party or the other (*The Tribune*)

kotha *or* (*feminine*) **kothi** *noun* **1** a donkey **2** *informal* a clumsy or inept person

> Watch out, you kotha, you nearly had my eye out!

kuli-shuti *noun* **1** free time **2** freedom; free rein

I've given my wife kuli-shuti when it comes to disciplining the children

kunjoos or kanjoos *noun informal* a miser

He wears the same socks five days in a row even though he's got a lakh in the bank. He's such a kunjoos

kunjoosi or kanjoosi *noun* stinginess; miserliness

I paid the extra in the end. I didn't want us all to be sitting in different parts of the theatre just because of my kunjoosi

kurta *noun* a loose shirt worn by both men and women, usually hanging down to the knees

Then she pointed to my V-necked kurta with its rolled-up sleeves. 'But you look just like us.' I knew then that I was to them what Bombay had been to me – something far more familiar than anticipated (*The Guardian*)

kuta or (*feminine*) kuti *noun* 1 a dog 2 *derogatory* an unpleasant or contemptible person

you're such a kuta! That girl's far too good for you!

kuwara *noun* a bachelor

It's great being a kuwara. I can come home whenever I like

kuwari *noun* a spinster

> to be a kuwari invites ridicule from my community

ladoo *noun* **1** a golf-ball-sized sweet: typically made from sugar, gram flour, and various other ingredients, esp nuts and raisins, fried in ghee and rolled into a ball **2** an affectionate term for a plump child

> in my particular Muslim community during feasts and wedding parties, we always serve rich sweetmeats, such as ladoo and barfi, before the main course (*The Independent*)

> I've not been blanking you, you ladoo! I had my phone nicked on Thursday night

lafanga *or* (*feminine*) **lafangi** *noun* a good-for-nothing; a troublemaker

> I did get in trouble a lot for being such a lafangi. Time and again my aunts would sit me down and explain that girls were meant to stay home and help their mother

lakh *noun* a unit equal to 100,000

> he has a lakh in the bank

> Nearly a lakh protestors turned up

lakshman rekha *noun* (in India) any agreed condition or limit, transgression of which supposedly has dire consequences

> After a bribery charge by its legislator against the Chief Minister sent the ruling coalition into a tizzy, the BJP today said it would work for drawing a 'lakshman rekha' with its partner (*Outlook India*)

Lakshmana is a character from Hindu mythology. When he went in search of his brother Rama he drew a line (rekha) around the home of Sita, his brother's wife, to protect her. Anyone attempting to cross the line would be consumed by flames.

langar *noun* **1** the name given to the free meal served after a Sikh service, usually in the communal kitchen of a gurdwara **2** the

communal kitchen itself

> It is a sacrament of Sikhism (laid down by the third Guru of the Sikhs, Sri Guru Amar Das Ji) that in every gurdwara a langar should be open and providing food for anyone at any time (*The Times*)

The *langar* is open to all people, regardless of their religion or social standing. Only vegetarian food is served so that it does not contravene the codes of any belief system. Open-air langars held during Sikh festivals are among the largest organized meals in the world, occasionally accommodating up to 100,000 people.

lathicharge *noun* (in South Asia) a charge by police wielding lathis: long sturdy bamboo canes used for crowd control

> The police resorted to lathicharge and opened four rounds of fire into the air to disperse the stone pelting mob (*Samachar*)

lehenga *noun* a long flowing skirt usually

embroidered or patterned and often worn by British Asian brides. It is nearly always worn in combination with a **choli** and a **dupatta**

> the winds of Westernization have led to the blending of tradition and modernity in the lehenga too (*IndiaFashion.com*)

Lollywood *noun* *informal* a name for the Pakistani film industry > *compare* **Bollywood**

> Now, Lollywood produces perhaps 40 films a year, compared to Bollywood's thousand or so releases (*The Guardian*)

Lollywood is so named because it originated in Lahore. Dwarfed by its Indian counterpart, it has gone into something of a decline compared with its successes in the 1970s and 80s.

love marriage *noun* a marriage in which the couple were in a romantic relationship together before they got married she left teacher-training college at 20 and had a love marriage at 21 to a fellow student (*The Golden Thread* by Zerbanoo Gifford)

maal *noun* goods

So, bhaji, what maal did you get at the shops?

machi-chips *noun* fish and chips

come on, everyone loves machi-chips

mama *or* **mamu** *noun* a younger brother of one's mother > *See* **Family Ties, page 50**

mami *noun* the wife of one's mother's younger brother > *See* **Family Ties, page 50**

mandir *noun* a Hindu place of worship

Hindus come from kilometres around to worship at the sparkling white mandir, which stands at the end of a pier in the sea (*The Toronto Sun*)

mangy *noun informal* **1** a mango **2** *offensive slang* a person who has recently immigrated from Pakistan into Britain

I told my parents I wouldn't ever get married to a mangy

The second, offensive, sense of the word depersonalizes the recently arrived immigrants, suggesting they have been imported en masse to Britain like a cargo of mangoes

mar-gaye *interjection* used to indicate one is in danger or liable for punishment or blame

> Mar-gaye! I forgot my mum's birthday. Again

In Hindi *mar-gaye* literally means 'dead-gone'.

masala *noun* 1 a mixture of spices ground into a paste, used in South Asian cookery *adjective informal* 2 spicy; melodramatic

> it was a typical masala film, you know – lots of action and romance

masala chai *noun* a hot drink popular in India and typically consisting of strong tea, milk, a sweetener such as sugar or honey, and any of a

variety of spices, esp cardamom, cinnamon, or
ginger

> recipes for masala chai can vary greatly from region to
> region, and even from family to family

masjid *noun* a Muslim place of worship; mosque

> The partnership has brought rabbis to speak at the
> masjid and members of the masjid have attended prayer
> services at the synagogue (*Pluralism.org*)

The word *Masjid* comes from Arabic and
means 'place of prostration'.

massar *noun* the husband of an elder sister of
one's mother
> *See* **Family Ties, page 50**

massi *noun* an elder sister of one's mother
> *See* **Family Ties, page 50**

masti *noun* indulgent fun or mischief

> I had such a good time at your party. It was total masti

matlab *sentence substitute* meaning

Your pedantic discourse on affairs of the heart does me
no good

Matlab?

Matlab, your know-it-all blethering about love is a load
of rubbish!

'matrimonial *noun* an advert placed in a
newspaper, magazine, on the internet, etc by
a person searching for a marriage partner for
himself or herself, or on behalf of someone else,
esp one of his or her children

> 'homely' means traditional, not 'ugly' as in the American
> sense of the word. (When I first read the matrimonials, I
> never understood why parents would advertise how ugly
> their children were) (*www.vij.com*)

mehenga, mehengi *or* **mehenge** *adjective*
expensive

> I avoid buying saris here, as they're a bit mehenge. A
> total rip-off, in fact

mehmaan *noun* a guest or guests

> mehmaan are so revered and feared in many British

Asian households, children are taught before they can walk to be on their best behaviour when in their presence

mehndi *noun* **1** the practice of painting designs on the hands, feet, etc, using henna, esp in the marriage preparations of a South Asian bride or groom **2** a temporary henna tattoo **3** the dye used

It was at the bride's family's house. We drank, ate, danced. She was decorated with the mehndi designs all over her hands and feet – rich, rich red, nearly maroon, like blood (*Exquisite Corpse* by Poppy Z Brite)

mela *noun* a cultural or religious fair or festival

the mela is one of many across the UK this month, featuring Indian food, crafts and fashion as well as cultural events (*The Belfast Telegraph*)

In Britain the word *mela* usually refers to a cultural fair in which artists, musicians, singers and dancers may perform. Games and food are also part of the experience. *Mela* comes from Sanskrit and means a 'gathering'. The Maha Kumb Mela is held

in Northern India every twelve years, and
is always the world's largest gathering of
people since the last one. At it, pilgrims
(some 70 million of them in 2001) come
to bathe in the River Ganges to purify
themselves of sin, and also to enjoy the
spectacle of one of the greatest shows on
earth.

mirchi *adjective* tasting hot and spicy

> I can't eat any more – it's too mirchi! It's burning my
> tongue!

mithai *noun* a type of South Asian sweet, usually
milk-based, often sent to relatives as gifts, esp at
Diwali (the festival of light celebrated by Hindus
and Sikhs)

> mithai are to South Asians as puddings are to the British

mixie *noun* *informal* (in India) a blender or food
processor

[the press campaign] is geared to the housewife in the middle-income segment who uses a 'mixie' on a daily basis (*The Hindu Business Line*)

miya *or* **mian** *noun* a husband

her miya is a lazy slob, but at least he's always smiling

mofussil *adjective* (in South Asia) provincial; away from major cities

At the military academy in Kakul raw cadets, many of them from mofussil schools, are taught to become 'gentlemen' in the Sandhurst manner (*Dawn.com*)

mooch *or* **mooche** *noun* *informal* (in South Asia) a moustache

my cousin-brother's growing a pencil mooch, but then he's always specialized in looking ridiculous

motu *or* **mota,** (*feminine*) **moti** *or* **moto** *noun* *derogatory* a fat person

I love you like a motu likes mithai!

Mumbaiyya (in India) *informal* | *adjective* **1** of or relating to Mumbai | *noun* **2** the dialect of Hindi spoken in Mumbai

> *Company* is of Mumbai, for Mumbai. The film is so full
> of Mumbaiyya slang and real-life situations that it might
> bounce over the heads of an audience from another city
> (*Rediff.com*)

musibat *noun* a problem

> there's always some sort of musibat when she gets
> involved

naan or **nahi** *sentence substitute* no

> Are you going out tonight? Nahi – I'm just going to
> watch telly

naashta *noun* breakfast

> I'm always late getting up so I never have time to have
> any naashta

nakra *noun, plural* **nakre** **1** dissembling
behaviour **2** a person who behaves in an affected
or dissembling manner

> Did you check out the nakre Meena was putting on? I
> don't think anyone fell for it

namaste or **namaskar** *interjection* a salutation

used both to greet people and say goodbye

> Namaste, fellow desis!

> I smiled at everyone I met, and said namaste

Namaste is also said when performing the *namas kar*, the traditional Indian salutation in which one places the palms together in front of the chest and bows.

nana *noun* one's maternal grandfather > *See* **Family Ties, page 50**

nani *noun* one's maternal grandmother > *See* **Family Ties, page 50**

naqli *adjective* (in South Asia) fake; not genuine

> That's a nice watch, man – I bet it's naqli though!

neta *noun* (in South Asia) a politician

> it is the usual story of our netas and babus colluding to spend our money on improving their own living conditions and those of their families and friends (*India Today*)

NRI *abbreviation for* non-resident Indian

> there has been a real rise in the number of banks that allow NRIs to send money back to their loved ones back in South Asia

paagal *adjective informal* crazy

> You paagal or something? Have you forgotten it's our anniversary?

paa-ji *informal* a brother, or someone considered to be like a brother

> Dev paa-ji, could you give me a lift to school, I'm running late

When used as a form of address, *paa-ji* is often said immediately after the name of the person being addressed.

page 3 people *noun* (in India) fashionable celebrities. *Often abbreviated to* **P3P**

> but love them or hate them, you can't miss them. The Page 3 People (P3P) are everywhere. Their plastic smiles glimmer more as they pout out of glossies (*The Tribune*)

paisa *noun, plural* **paise** money

if I had all the paise in the world I still wouldn't be happy without her

panga *noun* take panga to get into an argument or fight

I'm telling you now, you don't want to take panga with me!

parallel *adjective* (in South Asia) (of cinema) art-house; not mainstream

a small group of young, dedicated and committed visionaries have successfully created a large group of enthusiastic viewers of parallel cinema in Karachi (*Dawn.com*)

pendu *noun* *slang* a yokel

That guy's such a pendu. See how much oil he puts on his head?

phuphar *noun* the husband of an elder sister of one's father > *See* **Family Ties, page 50**

pind *noun* a village

Where's your pind, mate?

The literal meaning is 'village', but when said in Britain it jokily refers to the place where you come from, which could be a village, but could just as easily be a city.

praune *plural noun* guests

> Sorry, I can't make it to your party. Mum says we've got praune coming over

prepone *verb* (in South Asia) to bring (something) forward to an earlier time

> [The movie,] scheduled to release on July 7, has been preponed to June 16! In these days when films regularly get postponed by months, it is a bold and brave move by the producers and distributors (*Sify.com*)

The word is modelled on *postpone*. Although in context it would be readily understood by most English speakers it is current only in South Asia.

pua *noun* an elder sister of one's father > *See* **Family Ties, page 50**

pugree *or* **pug** *noun* a turban

> The pugree is more than mere headgear, a rudimentary and functional object to protect the wearer from the scorching heat or the biting cold (*India Profile*)

pukka *adjective* **1** properly or perfectly done, constructed, cooked, etc

> that's a pukka road they've laid done

2 genuine; authentic

> he's not even a pukka Indian

3 *informal* excellent

> it's the first time I've been to carnival and I thought it was pukka

pupi *noun* an Urdu term for the eldest sister of one's father > *See* **Family Ties, page 50**

pupr *noun* an Urdu term for the husband of one's father's eldest sister > *See* **Family Ties, page 50**

qawwali *noun* a form of devotional singing linked with those that practise Sufism, a sect of Islam on the magical 'Worlds Apart' the E Street Band is mixed with a Pakistani group singing qawwali (*The Times*)

rakhi *noun* a decorated string bracelet that a woman ties upon the wrist of a brother (or someone whom she considers to be like a brother) during Raksha Bandhan, the annual moveable festival dedicated to this practice, usually falling in August. In return the recipient pledges his lifelong protection

I love tying a rakhi on my five brothers because not only do I get their protection but they give me money too

Ranjha *noun* *informal* a male lover; a Romeo

my brother's a bit of a Ranjha with the ladies

Heer Ranjha is an epic Punjabi tale of two ill-starred lovers, Heer and Ranjha, whose tragic fate is similar to that of Romeo and Juliet. The most famous version was set down in verse by the Punjabi poet Waris Shah (1719-90) in 1766

rasmalai *noun* **1** an Indian dessert, made from cheese, milk, and nuts **2** *informal* a physically attractive woman

> Did you ask that rasmalai on a date or what?

sabzi *or* **sabji** *noun* **a** vegetables **b** a dish consisting of vegetables

> as a whole, milk, lentils, seasonal sabzi, and flour and wheat products are the most abundant foods, forming the basis of Pakistani cuisine

sala *noun* **1** the brother of one's wife **2** *derogatory* a fool or an idiot, used esp as a term of address > *See* **Family Ties, page 50**

It is unclear exactly how the word *sala* came to have its derogatory connotations when used as a term of address. One popular theory is that it was originally a stronger insult, implying that the speaker is sleeping with the target's sister. When British Asians use the term these days it generally doesn't mean anything stronger than 'idiot'. All the same, to people who aren't familiar with South Asian languages, this might seem like a rough deal for brothers-in-law as well as a recipe for disaster at family gatherings, but it is always unmistakeably clear from the context which sense is intended.

sali *noun* **1** the sister of one's wife **2** *informal* a (female) fool or idiot > *See* **Family Ties, page 50**

sanyasi *or* **sannyasi** *noun* a Hindu who has renounced all worldly possessions; an ascetic

> I once heard of millionaire who became a sannyasi

sardar *or* **sirdar** *noun* **1** a title given to the male head of any household (esp a Sikh one) and used before his name: *Sardar Pritam Singh* **2** a leader **3** any Punjabi man

> Did you see that sardar telling jokes on TV last night?

sari *or* **saree** *noun* the traditional dress of women of South Asia consisting of a very long narrow piece of cloth swathed elaborately around the body

> in one of the largest Asian communities in Britain, Sayeeda Warsi, a Conservative candidate, will celebrate St George's Day today by draping herself in a sari depicting the Union Jack (*The Times*)

sarkari *adjective* (in India) of or relating to government

> Believe it or not, there are people out there who have faith in things sarkari (*Business Today*)

sastha, sasthi *or* **sasthe** *adjective* cheap

> My brother looks so sastha in those shoes. They've got holes in them

sat-sri-akal *interjection* Punjabi and Sikh salutation said on meeting as well as on parting. It means literally 'eternal is the timeless lord'

> most Pakistani officials greeted the Indian Sikh Jatha with 'sat sri akal' on the Pakistan side and were appreciative of the fact that the Sikhs had made it to Pakistan despite all odds (*The Tribune of India*)

seedha-saadha *adjective* straightforward; ingenuous

> I'm very seedha-saadha, so you won't be getting any mixed messages from me

shaadi *noun* a wedding

> before the market got too crowded you could get four hundred bucks doing a big shaadi reception in a hotel ballroom near Heathrow (*Londonstani* by Gautam Malkani)

shabash *interjection* well done!; bravo!

> there aren't too many words in Hindi, Urdu, or Punjabi that express praise, but *shabash* is one of them

shaitan *noun* **1** (in Islamic belief) Satan **2** any evil spirit **3** a vicious person **4** a mischievous person, esp a badly behaved child

> my massi's little boy is a shaitan – he always gets what he wants

shalwar *or* **salwar** *noun* a pair of loose-fitting trousers tapering to a narrow fit around the ankles, often worn with a kameez the attempt to divide the nation into those wearing shalwar and those wearing jeans is absurd and dangerous (*The Daily Times*)

sharaabi *noun* a drunkard

dad came home like a sharaabi last night. Mum had a fit

sharm *noun* shame

If you have any sharm left you will apologise this minute!

sherwani *noun* a man's long coat-like garment that is often embroidered and is usually worn over a shalwar kameez, esp on formal occasions

the general's sherwani flapped in the wind as he inspected the troops

shukriya *interjection* thank you

I want to say shukriya to everyone who helped out

sidha *adjective* straight

trust me, I've got directions. It's sidha from here

soft corner *noun* (in South Asia) a sentimental fondness; a soft spot always behaving like an elderly teacher and guide, he had a soft corner for women writers and always encouraged them (*Dawn.com*)

sohniya *or* (*feminine*) **sohniye** *noun* a term of address between good friends

Hey sohniya! where have you been, man?

stepney *noun* (in India) **1** a spare wheel for a motor vehicle **2** *figurative* a spare of anything **3** *slang* a woman with whom one is having an affair; a mistress

scooters are easily repaired, they usually come with a stepney, cheap spares and are dependable (*The Tribune*)

Sooner or later, you decide to go in for a newer PC. But the resale value of your old machine is so low, that you prefer to retain it as a 'Stepney' (*The Hindu*)

Her husband had two 'stepneys'. Life in purdah left her unaware of her partner's ways for 10 years (*WLUML.org*)

The *Stepney* was originally a particular type of spare tyre which could be clamped around the burst one. Stepney refers to Stepney

Street in Llanelli, the place where it was manufactured. The term was once common in Britain and other English-speaking countries around the world but has now died out everywhere except Malta and South Asia where it now means simply a spare wheel, or indeed a spare anything – even, rather insultingly it must be said, a mistress, or 'spare' woman.

supari *noun* (in India) a contract for an assassination

> [there are] inconsistencies in the police version. For instance, the police initially claimed that the murder was plotted at a party on June 12, but now say it was planned in May this year. Also, the 'supari' amount varies from 25 lakh rupees to 40 lakh rupees (*India Today*)

tamasha *noun* **1** (in South Asia) a show; entertainment **2** *informal* a commotion, esp an embarrassing one in a public place

> I'm sure she just wants to make a tamasha out of herself

RANJHA!

tameez *noun* manners; respect

> You call me everything under the sun and then accuse me of not addressing you with tameez?

tantric *noun* (in South Asia) a magician; holy man

> and there is an element of stereotyping with India continuing to be a land of tantrics and snakes and what have you (*The Hindu*)

teek-hoon, teek-hain *or* **teek-a** *interjection* okay

> 'Make sure you turn up on time for that interview.' 'Teek-hain'

thaiya *noun* an elder brother of one's father > *See* **Family Ties, page 50**

thaiyee *noun* the wife of an elder brother of one's father > *See* **Family Ties, page 50**

thapparh *noun* a slap

> An so I carried on standin up for her, carried on defendin her ways. Right up until Hardjit raised his hand as if he was gonna give me a thapparh across the face (*Londonstani* by Gautam Malkani)

tikka *noun* **1** > *another word for* **tilak** **2** a small spicy potato fritter

tilak *noun* a coloured spot worn by Hindus, esp on the forehead, often indicating membership of a religious sect, caste, etc, or, in the case of a woman, marital status

> His trademark tilak glistening on his forehead, the dimunitive CEO of the embattled scooter manufacturer waves his hand over the Korean mean machines. 'You tell me, which motorbikes are better?' (*Business Today*)

timepass (in India) | *noun* **1 a** a hobby **b** any mildly diverting activity | *adjective* **2** entertaining enough to pass the time

> What do you do for timepass?

> this website provides plenty of timepass material

too *adverb* (in South Asian speech, especially in the phrase **too good**) very

> That Flintoff – he's too good, innit?

In Britain, the 'too' is said in a heavy Indian

accent to intensify the effect.

tutta-futta or (*feminine*) **tutti-futti** *adjective*
informal broken; out of order

> my car is all tutti-futti

ullu-ka-patha or (*feminine*) **ullu-ki-pathi** *noun*
derogatory a fool; a good-for-nothing

> there's a bit of a difference between calling someone an
> ulla-ka-patha and saying their sister's sleeping around
> (forum on *Chowk.com*)

> *Ullu-ka-patha* literally means 'son of an owl'.

ulta pulta *adjective* (in South Asia) upside down;
topsy-turvy

> according to Eurostat, the EU's statistics agency, by 2050
> Europe's population will have fallen by around 1.5%, or 7
> million people. In Pakistan, it is all ulta pulta, all upside
> down. How many millions will we have added to our
> country? (*Dawn.com*)

uncle-ji *noun* a name and form of address for a
man from the generation older than oneself

> uncle-ji, there's a phone call for you

So then this uncle-ji walks over and starts coming on to me. I couldn't believe it. I mean, he looked like my dad!

undertrial *noun* (in South Asia) a prisoner awaiting or undergoing trial

> in a sensational jailbreak, 13 undertrials escaped from the court complex of the high-security Tihar Central Jail on Wednesday (*The Hindu*)

updation *noun* (in South Asia) the process of updating

> please contact or write to your branch for updation of this information (*StateBankofIndia.com*)

vaah vaah *or* **waah waah** *interjection informal* an exclamation of admiration, esp for something aesthetically pleasing

> Vaah vaah! That music is beautiful, what is it?

wheatish *adjective* (of a South Asian person's complexion) the colour of wheat; neither dark nor very fair

> beautiful doctor's daughter with wheatish complexion

seeks suitable match (from an internet matrimonial)

The term was perhaps coined in an attempt to circumvent newspapers' banning of certain explicit colour-related terms in matrimonials.

would-be *noun* (in India) a person who is engaged to be married

> My blood group is A+ and my would-be's is A-. Will it make any complication in our married life? (from a post on an Indian forum on *BloodGivers.org*)

yaar *noun informal* a friend: often used between males in direct address

> Where's The Party, Yaar? (*The name of a 2003 film directed by Benny Mathews*)

yatri *noun* (in South Asia) a voyager; a pilgrim

> they have assembled a 40-strong convoy to take the yatris to the shrine (*Dawn.com*)

zindabaad *interjection* long live (freedom)!

> Scotland zindabaad!

OLD HINGLISH

South Asian words have been a part of British life since the late 1500s. They were brought back by the Elizabethan traders who first established direct links between Britain and the South Asian subcontinent. Back then these strange new terms were as exciting and outlandish as the spices and fabrics that travelled with them. Nowadays though, some of these expressions have become so commonplace it often comes as a surprise to remember the remarkable journey they have made to take their place in today's English.

The following pages contain a list of such words, and a brief history for each. A couple, with their odd spellings, still retain something vaguely 'Eastern' about them, but most of these once-exotic terms are now as British as roast beef and Yorkshire pudding, or (as there's an excellent case for putting it), as chicken tikka masala.

bandanna *or* **bandana** *noun* In the 18th century, when this word was first introduced into English, it referred specifically to silk handkerchiefs that had been tie-dyed: from Hindi *bāndhnū* 'tie-dyeing', from *bāndhnā* 'to tie', from Sanskrit *bandhnāti* 'he ties'.

bangle *noun* 19th century: from Hindi *bangrī*

Blighty *noun* *Brit* *slang* This word, which came to represent 'home' for generations of British troops serving overseas orginally meant precisely the opposite for Hindi-speaking Indians, to whom Britain seemed very foreign indeed. 20th century: from Hindi *bilāyatī* 'foreign land', England, from Arabic *wilāyat* 'country', from *waliya* 'he rules'.

bobbery *noun* (noisy commotion) 19th century: from Hindi *bāp re*, a popular expression of dismay or surprise, literally 'oh father!'

cheetah *noun* 18th century: from Hindi *cītā*,

from Sanskrit *citrakāya* 'tiger', from *citra* 'bright', 'speckled' + *kāya* 'body'

chillum *noun* (cannabis pipe) This word, which many people assume is modern slang and has something to do with the relaxing connotations of the verb 'to chill', has actually been established in English for a respectable two hundred years. 18th century: from Hindi *cilam*, from Persian *chilam*

chit *or* **chitty** (note or voucher) 18th century: from earlier *chitty*, from Hindi *cittha* 'note', from Sanskrit *citra* 'marked' or 'coloured'

cot *noun* 17th century: from Hindi *khāt* 'bedstead', from Sanskrit *khátvā*

cummerbund *or* **kummerbund** *noun* 17th century: from Hindi *kamarband*, from Persian, from *kamar* 'loins', 'waist' + *band* 'band'

cushy *adjective* *informal* 20th century: from

Hindi *khush* 'pleasant', from Persian *khōsh*

> *Cushy* is thought to share South Asian roots
> with *cushty*. The latter, Del Boy's favourite
> pronouncement, is a corruption of a Romani
> word whose incorporation into mainstream
> English was helped along first by the
> popularity of its older Hindi soundalike, then
> by Peckham's most famous entrepreneur

dekko *noun Brit slang* (esp in the phrase **take a
dekko at**) 19th century: from Hindi *dekho!* 'look!'
from *dekhnā* 'to see'

dinghy 19th century: from Hindi or Bengali *dingi*
'little boat', from *dingā* 'boat'

doolally *adjective slang* 19th century: from
military slang. The original version, was *doolally
tap*, from *Deolali*, a town near Bombay, the
location of a military sanatorium + Hindustani *tap*
'fever'

dungarees *noun* 17th century: *dungaree* was a type of coarse Indian cotton from which the overalls now beloved of workmen, pregnant ladies, and children's TV presenters were first made. From Hindi *dungrī*, after *Dungrī*, district of Bombay, where this fabric originated

ganja *noun* (potent form of cannabis) 19th century: from Hindi *gājā*, from Sanskrit *grñja*

guru *noun* Over the years this term has acquired a rather disparaging tone in English, but when it first appeared it carried a certain mystical gravitas, and was not lightly applied until the last century. 17th century: from Hindi *gurū*, from Sanskrit *guruh* 'weighty'

gymkhana *noun* Although the term now specifically refers to an equestrian event, esp one in which children take part, it originally described an area set aside for any competitive sporting activity, and hence the sports meet itself. 19th century: from Hindi *gend-khānā,* literally 'ball house' (a court for racquet sports), from *khāna* 'house'; influenced by GYMNASIUM

kebab *noun* 17th century: via Urdu from Arabic *kabāb* 'roast meat'

loot *noun* and *verb* 19th century: from Hindi *lūt*

punch *noun* (the drink) 17th century: perhaps from Hindi *pānch,* from Sanskrit *pañca* 'five', as the beverage originally included five ingredients, often listed as water, tea, lemon, sugar, and arrack

pundit *noun* Like *guru,* the label of *pundit* is now applied rather more casually than it was when it first arrived. 17th century: from Hindi *pandit,* from Sanskrit *pandita* 'learned man', from *pandita* 'learned'

puttee *or* **putty** *noun* (strip of cloth worn wound

around lower legs, esp in military uniforms) 17th century: from Hindi *pattī* 'bandage' from Sanskrit *pattikā*, from *patta* 'band of cloth'

pyjamas *or* US **pajamas** *noun* 19th century: via Persian or Urdu from Persian *pāï, pāÿ* foot, leg (because the term originally referred only to light loose trousers) + *jāmah* 'clothing' or 'garment'

seersucker *noun* (the light fabric) 18th century: from Hindi *śīrśakar*, from Persian *shīr o shakkar*, literally 'milk and sugar', because the material was originally striped with alternating bands of different textures

shampoo *noun* and *verb* When it first arrived in English the verb *to shampoo* meant simply to massage (the body): it wasn't until the late 19th century that it began to assume its present-day noun and verb senses. 18th century: from Hindi *chāmpo*, from *chāmpnā* 'to knead'

thug *noun* The Thugs were an organized cult of professional robbers and assassins whose grisly speciality was strangling their victims. They operated in India from around the 13th century until their practice, known as *thuggee,* was finally stamped out by the British in the 1830s. 19th century: from Hindi *thag* 'thief', from Sanskrit *sthaga* 'scoundrel', from *sthagati* 'to conceal'

toddy *noun* (the hot alcoholic drink) 17th century: from Hindi *tārī* 'juice of the palmyra palm' (because a similarly intoxicating drink was prepared from fermented palmyra sap), from *tār* 'palmyra palm', from Sanskrit *tāra*

tom-tom *noun* (the drum) 17th century: from Hindi *tamtam,* of imitative origin